Insects
Sticker Book

Anthony Wootton

Illustrated by Phil We...

Edited by Sarah Khan
Designed by Leonard le Rolland
Consultant: Dr Margaret Rostron

How to use this book

There are over a hundred insects in this book. Using the descriptions and pictures, match each sticker with the right insect. If you need help, a list at the back of the book tells you which page each description is on and which sticker goes with it. You can also use the book as a spotter's handbook to make a note of the insects you've seen.

Here are some of the words used to describe insects:

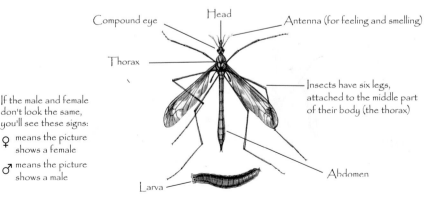

Compound eye — Head — Antenna (for feeling and smelling)

Thorax

Insects have six legs, attached to the middle part of their body (the thorax)

If the male and female don't look the same, you'll see these signs:

♀ means the picture shows a female

♂ means the picture shows a male

Larva

Abdomen

Many insects have young called larvae (singular: larva), that look different from the adults. Butterfly and moth larvae are called caterpillars. Other insects have young called nymphs that look like small, wingless adults.

Butterflies

Wall brown

Brown butterfly with spots that look like eyes on front and back wings. Often in dry, open spaces. 44–46mm

WHEN ....

WHERE ....

Wall brown

Brown argus

Brown argus

Brown wings with orange marks near edges. Males are said to smell of chocolate when trying to attract females. 28–30mm

WHEN ....

WHERE ....

Clouded yellow

Clouded yellow

Pale orange wings with dark edges. Flies to Britain from southern Europe in spring. 58–62mm

WHEN ....

WHERE ....

Purple hairstreak

Flies around oak trees. Males have purplish wings with black borders; females have black wings with purple streaks on front wings. 36–39mm

WHEN ....

WHERE ....

Purple hairstreak

Marbled white

Marbled black and white wings. Found all over Europe; common in southern England. 53–58mm

WHEN ....

WHERE ....

Marbled white

Brimstone

Large. Male is yellow; female is pale greenish white. Not found in Scotland, but is common in the rest of Britain. 58–62mm

WHEN ....

WHERE ....

Brimstone

♂

Small tortoiseshell

Common throughout the UK. Brightly patterned wings with blue half-moons along edges. 50–56mm

WHEN ....

WHERE ....

Small tortoiseshell

Pearl-bordered fritillary

Black markings on orange-brown wings. Pearly spots underneath. Found all over Britain. 42–46mm

WHEN ....

WHERE ....

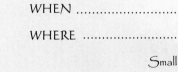

Peacock

Peacock

Adults hibernate in winter. Large, brightly coloured wings with eye-like markings. 62–68mm

WHEN ....

WHERE ....

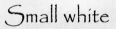

Small white

♀

Small white

Common white butterfly. Flits around gardens, especially near cabbages. 48–50mm

WHEN ....

WHERE ....

Pearl-bordered fritillary

Moths

Puss moth

Caterpillar

Puss moth

Pale pink and grey.
Common throughout
Britain. Caterpillar pokes
thin red "whips" out of tail
when alarmed. 65–80mm

WHEN ....

WHERE ....

Emperor moth ♀

Emperor moth

Yellowish, eye-like wing spots.
Females are grey and white. Males
are smaller, with a more reddish tinge,
orange back wings, and more feathery
antennae. Female: 70mm, male: 55mm

WHEN ....

WHERE ....

Lobster moth

Claw-like tail

Lobster moth

Gets its name from its
caterpillar's tail end, which looks
like a lobster's claw. Adult is a dull,
grey-brown colour. 65–70mm

WHEN ....

WHERE ....

Hummingbird hawk-moth

Hummingbird hawk-moth

Hovers over flowers, beating its wings like
a hummingbird. Brown front wings and
orange back wings. 45mm

WHEN ....

WHERE ....

Peach blossom

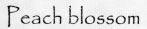

Peach blossom

Found in woodlands. So
named because of the pink
spots on its brown front
wings. 35mm

WHEN ....

WHERE ....

Clifden nonpareil or blue underwing

Rare, but might be spotted in eastern and southern England. Mottled grey front wings. Dark back wings with pale blue stripes around them. 90mm

WHEN ....

WHERE ....

Clifden nonpareil

Red underwing

Flashes red and black back wings when threatened. Colour of front wings matches tree bark. 80mm

WHEN ....

WHERE ....

Red underwing

Silver Y

Dull-coloured. Front wings have white markings shaped like the letter "Y". 40mm

WHEN ....

WHERE ....

Silver Y

Vapourer

Males have brown wings. Females only have wing stubs, so can't fly. Found all over Britain. 35mm

WHEN ....

WHERE ....

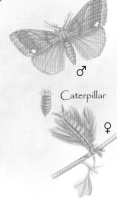

Vapourer

♂

Caterpillar

♀

Oak eggar

♂

Oak eggar

Brown wings with yellow edges. White spot on each front wing. Males have feather-like antennae. 50–65mm

WHEN ....

WHERE ....

Moths

Garden tiger

Orange back wings with black spots. Mottled brown and cream front wings. Caterpillars called woolly bears. 60–70mm

WHEN ....

WHERE ....

Garden tiger

Woolly bear

Ghost moth

Males are white. Females have browner wings, so are better camouflaged. 50–60mm

WHEN ....

WHERE ....

Ghost moth ♂

Swallow-tailed moth

Pale-coloured. Large petal-shaped wings make it look like a butterfly. Flies in a weak, fluttering way. 56mm

WHEN ....

WHERE ....

Swallow-tailed moth

Lappet moth

Veined brown wings, held overlapping, so look like bunches of dry leaves. Caterpillars have flaps called lappets along their sides. 60–70mm

WHEN ....

WHERE ....

Lappet moth

Lappet

Wood tiger

Brown and cream patterns. Seen in open woodland, on hillsides and heaths. 35–40mm

WHEN ....

WHERE ....

Wood tiger

Death's head hawk-moth

Rare. So named because of skull-like markings on thorax. Front wings patterned brown; back wings light brown with darker stripes. Lays eggs on potato leaves. 100–125mm

WHEN ....

WHERE ....

Death's head
hawk-moth

Cinnabar

Cinnabar

Flies short distances by day. Red back wings. Dark brown front wings marked with two spots and two red streaks. Yellow and black caterpillars can be seen on ragwort plants. 40–45mm

WHEN ....

WHERE ....

Six-spot burnet

Six red spots on each front wing. Red back wings warn birds that it tastes bad. 35mm

WHEN ....

WHERE ....

Six-spot
burnet

Eyed
hawk-moth

Eyed hawk-moth

Large eye-like markings on pink and brown back wings. Shows back wings quickly to frighten off enemies. 75–80mm

Forester

Forester

Green front wings and pale back wings. Often flies over meadows in summer. 25–27mm

WHEN ....

WHERE ....

WHEN ....

WHERE ....

Beetles

Seven-spot ladybird

Red with seven black spots. Very common in Britain. Most likely to be seen on sunny days. 6–7mm

WHEN ....

WHERE ....

Seven-spot
ladybird

Stag beetle

Largest beetle in Britain. Males have purplish wing cases, black head and legs, and long, antler-like jaws. 25–75mm

WHEN ....

WHERE ....

Stag beetle

♂

Cockchafer

Cockchafer or maybug

Flies into lit windows in early summer. Black head, brown wing cases. Furry underneath thorax. 25–30mm

WHEN ....

WHERE ....

Rose chafer

Front of thorax very round. Almost square wing cases. Green. Found all over Britain. 14–20mm

WHEN ....

WHERE ....

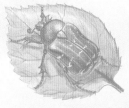

Rose chafer

Musk beetle

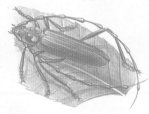

Musk beetle

Very long, green body and even longer beady antennae. 20–32mm

WHEN ....

WHERE ....

Water beetle

Water beetle

Common in lakes and rivers. Brown or black. Lays eggs on water plants. 7–8mm

WHEN ....

WHERE ....

Cardinal beetle

Cardinal beetle

Three kinds in Europe. This one has a long, red body, and antennae with branches along them. Found on flowers and under bark. 15–17mm

WHEN ....

WHERE ....

Click beetle

Wireworm

Glow-worm

Females have long, brown wingless bodies. Glowing tails attract males. Male: 15mm, female: 20mm

WHEN ....

WHERE ....

Glow-worm

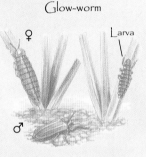

♀   Larva

♂

Click beetle or skip-jack

Can flip its body into the air with a loud click. Many types. This one has a sleek, green body and branched antennae. Larvae called wireworms. 14–18mm

WHEN ....

WHERE ....

Great diving beetle

Larva

Great diving beetle

Lives in lakes and ponds. Black body with light brown edges. Brown legs and antennae. 30–35mm

WHEN ....

WHERE ....

Green tiger beetle

A fierce, sharp-jawed hunter. Common in open woodlands and sandy areas in early summer. Larvae make burrows, and lie in wait to ambush ants. 12–15mm

WHEN ....

WHERE ....

Green tiger beetle

Larva

Beetles

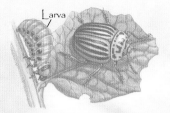

Larva

Wasp beetle

Looks like a wasp, with yellow stripes along its brown body. Flies around flowers on sunny days. 15mm

WHEN ....

WHERE ....

Wasp beetle

Colorado beetle

Colorado beetle

Causes serious damage to potato crops. Rounded body. Dark and light brown stripes along wing cases. 10–12mm

WHEN ....

WHERE ....

Bloody-nosed beetle

Bloody-nosed beetle

Produces a smelly red liquid from its mouth when threatened. Eats leaves. Round, black wing cases are joined together, so it can't fly. 10–20mm

WHEN ....

WHERE ....

Nut weevil

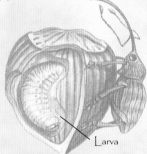

Larva

Green tortoise beetle

Looks a little like a tiny tortoise when its legs and antennae are hidden. Spiny larvae carry their own droppings and dead skins in their forked tails, to put off hungry enemies. 6–8mm

WHEN ....

WHERE ....

Nut weevil

Females use their long snouts to bore into hazelnuts, then lay eggs in the holes. Larvae grow inside the nuts, eating the kernels. 10mm

WHEN ....

WHERE ....

Green tortoise beetle

Larva

Devil's coach horse or cocktail beetle

Often in gardens. Can squirt foul-smelling liquid from its tail at enemies. 25–30mm

WHEN ....

WHERE ....

Devil's coach horse

Great silver water beetle

Great silver water beetle

Britain's largest water beetle. Large, black body with hairy back legs. Claws on front legs. 37–48mm

WHEN ....

WHERE ....

Horned dung beetle or minotaur beetle

Black with broad, ribbed wing cases, and tough, thick legs. Large horns around head. 12–18mm

WHEN ....

WHERE ....

Horned dung beetle

Death watch beetle

Eats wood in timber buildings. Makes a ticking noise, knocking its head on walls as it tunnels through wood. Ticking was once thought to mean someone was about to die. 7–10mm

WHEN ....

WHERE ....

Death watch beetle

Rove beetle

Different kinds. This one has red eyes and legs, a red section in the thorax and a long, black tail. Eats dead animals. 20mm

WHEN ....

WHERE ....

Rove beetle

Bugs

Water boatman or backswimmer

Swims on its back, with the tips of its legs clinging to underside of water surface. Back legs shaped like paddles and fringed with hairs. 15mm

WHEN ....

WHERE ....

Water boatman

Water cricket

Long legs and dark body with two light brown stripes along it. Seen on surface of still water. Eats insects and spiders. 6–7mm

WHEN ....

WHERE ....

Water cricket

Black and red froghopper

Red and black stripes. Jumps when disturbed. Most froghopper nymphs produce blobs of froth, known as cuckoo-spit. 9–10mm

WHEN ....

WHERE ....

Black and red froghopper

Pond skater

Small, with very long legs and thin bodies. Skates with middle legs, uses back legs as rudders and catches prey with front legs. 8–10mm

WHEN ....

WHERE ....

Pond skater

Saucer bug

Saucer bug

Lives among plants at the bottom of muddy pools and canals. Short legs. Front legs are rounded and very sharp. Beware of sharp, stabbing jaws. 12–16mm

WHEN ....

WHERE ....

1

2

3

4

5

6

7

8   ♀

Ovipositor

9

10

11

12

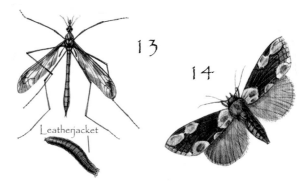

13

Leatherjacket

14

15

Larva

16

17

19

18

22

20

21

23

24

Wireworm

25

26

27

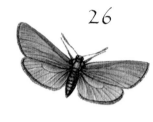

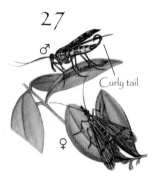

♂

Curly tail

♂

28

29

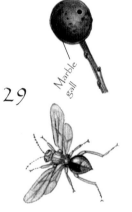

Marble gall

♂

30

♀

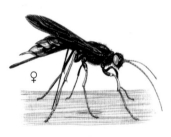

31

33

34

32

Larva

♂

35

36

37

Caterpillar

38

39

40

Pot

41

42

43

44

♂

Caterpillar

♀

45

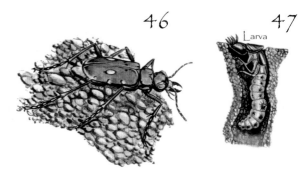
46

47
Larva

48

49
Egg
mat

51

52

53

54

55
Breathing
tube

Claw-like
tail
56

50

57

58
♂

59
♀

60

61

62

63
♀

64
♂

65
Woolly bear

66
Larva

67

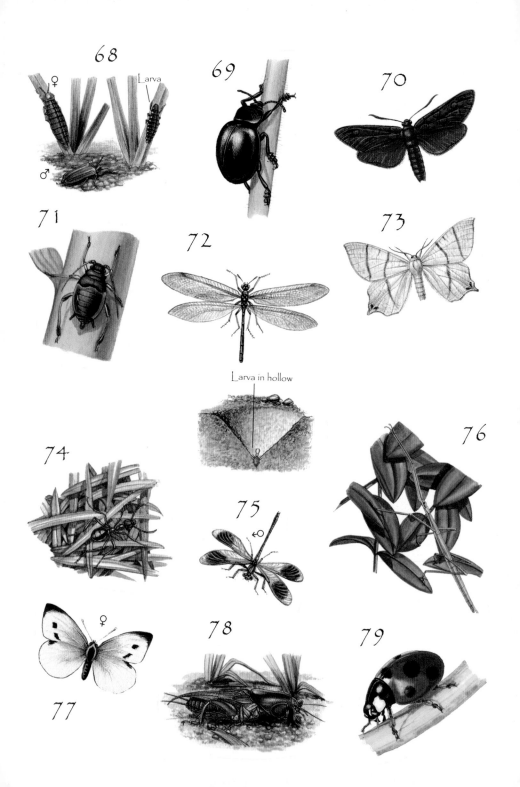

68

♀

Larva

♂

69

70

71

72

73

Larva in hollow

74

75

76

←o

77

♀

78

79

80

81

82

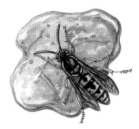

83

84

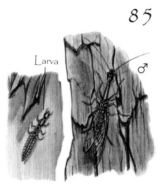

85

Larva

♂

86

87

88

89